CW01465663

A CHRISTMAS DREAM

.

A
CHRISTMAS
DREAM

BY
PAUL ISHERWOOD

Copyright © 2024 by Paul Isherwood

All rights reserved.

No portion of this book may be reproduced in any form without written permission from the publisher or author, except as permitted by copyright law.

Contents

Preface

The spirit of Christmas has always held a special kind of magic—a light that warms even the coldest of days and reminds us of what matters most.

In this little tale, I hope to share a story that brings comfort and joy. Though it begins with sorrow, it is a journey toward rediscovery—a quiet miracle that rekindles love, connection, and hope.

May this story be a gift for you this season, a gentle reminder of the enduring magic of Christmas.

~ P. I.

December 2024

1

A Box of Memories

Oliver had always loved Christmas. He loved the decorations, the music, the movies, and the cosy feeling of it all. But this year, it felt impossible to enjoy any of it.

He could tell that his mum had made an extra special effort this year. The Christmas tree in the living room was a masterpiece of twinkling lights and glittering ornaments. Garlands framed the fireplace, and the fire, lovingly tended, filled the house with its comforting glow.

Oliver wanted to enjoy it, to love it like he always had but he couldn't. The emptiness in his chest made it feel unreachable, like a melody he couldn't quite remember.

As he sat on the floor of his bedroom, leaning against the edge of his bed, a feeling—a kind of gentle stillness—settled over him. His gaze was drawn towards the window. Snowflakes had begun to fall, delicate and shimmering in the glow of the streetlights. The world outside was transforming, the rooftops and gardens turning white, as if Christmas itself had decided to make an appearance.

It was the kind of moment that should have filled him with wonder. A white Christmas was what he'd always dreamed of. But this year, it felt cruel. The snow had come, but the joy it should have brought felt impossibly far away.

"Ollie! Ollie! It's snowing!" Ben's shout rang up the stairs, bursting with excitement.

For a moment, Oliver stayed where he was, staring out at the snow. It was beautiful, magical even. Any other year, he would have raced outside with Ben, laughing and trying to catch snowflakes on his tongue.

But this year, he couldn't bring himself to move. The snow could fall, the magic could swirl outside, but it felt distant—out of reach. It didn't seem fair for it to snow now, when everything inside him felt so empty.

With a sigh, Oliver turned away from the window and sank to the floor, his gaze falling on the battered cardboard box in front of him. He hadn't opened it since summer, when Grandma's funeral had left them all raw and quiet. Now, with Christmas only days away, the thought of her absence felt like a heavy weight pressing down on his chest.

He reached for the box that held his most precious memories, his fingers lingering on the worn edges. Slowly, he lifted the lid, as if the memories inside might spill out and drown him. But he had to risk it. Maybe there was something inside that would make him feel just a little better—something that might bring Grandma back, even for just a moment.

The first thing he saw was the photograph—his favourite one. Grandma, her silver hair tucked under a woolly hat, stood beside him in the snow, both of them grinning with pink cheeks. He remembered that day so clearly. They'd spent the morning in the village, first building a snowman on the village green, which was covered in the best snow. Afterward, they'd made their way to Miss Sophia's bookshop, where Miss Sophia herself had greeted them at the door, her kind eyes smiling behind her spectacles.

"Well, if it isn't my favourite snow sculptors!" she'd said, pulling out a tray of freshly baked Christmas cookies.

Grandma had laughed, her cheeks pink from the cold. "Almost as good as mine," she'd teased, taking a cookie and passing one to Oliver. Miss Sophia had chuckled, rolling her eyes before flashing a warm smile at Oliver. Grandma and Miss Sophia had been old friends, and their playful banter was as comforting as

the crackling fire inside. They spent a perfect time in the shop, just enough to browse a few shelves of festive stories and sip hot chocolate by the fire. It was one of those magical moments—simple, warm, and full of love
.

But now, as he looked at the photo, his chest ached. It wasn't just the picture itself that brought the heaviness—it was what it stood for: those years when his family had felt whole, when his grandma and grandad had been there.

It had always been the five of them. Grandma and Grandad. Mum, Oliver, and Ben.

Oliver set the photo aside and reached deeper into the box, pulling out another picture. This one was older, the corners curled and soft. It showed his dad holding him as a baby, a broad smile on his face.

He stared at the photo through the tears that suddenly pricked his eyes.

Oliver had been too young to remember much about him, but there was a feeling in his memory of a warm hug and his dad's deep laugh. After his dad died,

Mum had done her best, but she'd needed to work full time to keep them afloat. Grandma had been the one who picked up the pieces, smoothing the edges of their broken world.

She'd done it so seamlessly, so lovingly, that Oliver had never felt like he was missing anything. She was the one who baked biscuits, read bedtime stories, and made every Christmas magical. She'd taught him how to roll out gingerbread dough, how to string lights on a tree, and how to make a proper mug of hot chocolate.

Grandma was always there.

And now she wasn't.

He brushed his thumb over the edge of the photo, then placed it gently beside the first, as if the two belonged together. Reaching deeper into the box, his fingers brushed against something small and familiar—the little snowman ornament they'd made years ago. It was simple yet perfect—crafted from a Christmas bauble covered in soft cotton wool.

As he held the snowman now, the memory came flooding back—a special time with his grandma. They had gone into the garden to find tiny twigs for his arms, and somehow his grandma had managed to paint on the kindest snowman face. He remembered the feel of the soft cotton wool in his tiny hands as they carefully stuck it together to make the snowman. He could still picture the way they had both admired the finished ornament together. And in that memory, he heard her voice as clearly as if she were in the room: "Perfect, Ollie. Just like magic."

A lump rose in his throat. He held on to the snowman, its cotton-wool body soft and fragile in his hands, and he slumped back against his bed. The silence in the room felt heavy, pressing down on him.

He wasn't sure how long he sat there, wrapped in the quiet ache of it all, until a voice broke through the stillness.

"Oliver?" Ben's voice came from the other side of the door, hesitant but hopeful.

Oliver didn't answer.

Ben knocked once, softly. "Mum and I are about to watch Elf. Do you want to come?"

For a second, Oliver almost said yes. But then the photograph flashed in his mind again—Grandma's smile, her hand resting on his shoulder—and the ache in his chest returned, sharp and bitter.

"Not now," he mumbled, keeping his eyes on the box.

There was a pause. Then the sound of Ben's footsteps retreating down the stairs.

Oliver leaned back against the bed, staring at the ceiling. The laughter from downstairs felt far away now, muffled and faint. He hated how lonely the house felt without Grandma's voice filling the rooms, without the warmth she brought to every corner of their lives.

No matter what Mum or Ben did, it could never be the same. Christmas without Grandma felt like trying to finish a puzzle with a missing piece.

His gaze drifted back to the box. It hadn't always made him feel this way. Once, it had been a treasure chest—a collection of his happiest memories. And just like that, one of those memories bubbled to the surface, vivid as if it had happened yesterday. He was six again, his feet dangling from a chair at the kitchen table. The air smelled of cinnamon and nutmeg, warm and sweet, as though Christmas itself was baking in the o ven.

Grandma bustled around the kitchen, her apron dusted with flour. "Now, Ollie," she said, setting a tray of gingerbread men on the counter, "what kind of house do you think they'd like to live in? Big and fancy? Or snug and cosy?"

"Snug!" Oliver declared. "With a big chimney for Santa."

She laughed, a sound that warmed him even more than the oven's heat. "Snug it is."

They worked together for hours, building and decorating the gingerbread house. Grandma's hands were quick and steady, icing snow onto the roof, while Oliver's fingers smeared icing everywhere else. By the time they finished, he was as sticky as the candy canes lining the gingerbread path.

"There," Grandma said, stepping back with a smile. "A masterpiece. What do you think?"

"It's perfect," Oliver said.

Grandad's booming voice interrupted them from the doorway. "What's this, then? A gingerbread palace fit for a king?"

Grandma spun around, hands on her hips. "It's a snug little house, thank you very much."

Oliver laughed as Grandad plucked a candy cane off the counter and popped it into his mouth. "Quality control," he said with a wink. "Carry on, team. It's looking smashing."

Grandma rolled her eyes fondly, and Oliver grinned. The warmth in the kitchen, the laughter, the love—it felt like the whole world was glowing.

The thought of Grandad triggered a different memory, one where the kitchen felt quieter and dimmer.

It was three years later, and Oliver was older, sitting at the same kitchen table. The gingerbread house they'd just decorated was smaller, simpler. Grandad wasn't standing in the doorway anymore. He hadn't been for months.

Grandma's hands moved a little slower as she piped the icing, her smile softer, though just as kind. "Still a masterpiece," she'd said that year, but it didn't feel the same.

The light of the memory faded, leaving only the ache in Oliver's chest.

When Grandad passed, it had been hard, but Grandma had kept things together. She still made gingerbread, still told stories by the fire, still made sure the tree lights twinkled the way they always had. She was the glue that held them all together.

And now, without her, it felt like everything had fallen apart.

2

A Familiar Glow

That night, the house was unusually quiet. The soft hum of the heating and the faint creak of the floorboards were the only sounds as Oliver lay in bed, the snowman ornament he'd pulled from the box earlier resting in his hands. Its cotton-wool body and delicate twigs for arms felt strangely comforting, as if it carried the warmth of the memory.

He stared up at the ceiling, where faint shadows shifted and danced. His mind wandered back to the photo of his dad, to the gingerbread houses with

Grandma, to Grandad's booming laugh. Those times felt so far away now, as if they were part of another life.

"I wish you were here," he whispered into the darkness. His fingers tightened around the snowman. "I wish things could be the way they used to be."

The stillness of the room pressed down on him, heavy and quiet, as if the very air was listening. For a moment, it felt like nothing would happen—that his words would simply vanish into the emptiness.

Then, slowly, a warm glow began to fill the space. It started faintly, like the first light of dawn, soft and hesitant, but it grew brighter, wrapping around him like a blanket. The faint scent of cinnamon and freshly baked gingerbread drifted through the air, stirring something deep within him.

Oliver sat up, his heart racing. "Mum?" he called hesitantly, but there was no answer.

The glow coalesced at the foot of his bed, and a familiar figure emerged from the light. Her silver hair curled softly around her face, her smile warm and bright. She looked just as she had in his happiest memories, her favourite red cardigan draped over her shoulders, her hands clasped in front of her.

"Grandma?" Oliver's voice cracked.

She stepped closer, her eyes sparkling. "Hello, my darling boy."

Oliver froze, his breath caught in his throat. He blinked hard, convinced he must be dreaming. "Grandma? How... how are you here? You're..." His voice trailed off.

"Dead," she said gently, sitting on the edge of the bed. Her voice was soft and comforting. "But I'm not really gone, Ollie. I'm here because you need me, and sometimes, dreams are the best way for love to find its way back."

Oliver stared at her, unsure whether to laugh, cry, or run to her. "How is this happening?" he managed to ask instead.

Her expression softened. "It's because of the strength of the desire in your heart," she said. "You've called me here, Ollie. Christmas has always been such a special time for you, but this year..." She reached out and brushed a strand of hair from his forehead. "This year, you've closed your heart to it."

"It doesn't feel the same anymore," Oliver said, his voice barely above a whisper. "Not without you."

"Oh, Ollie," Grandma said, taking his hand in hers. "I know how much you miss me. And I miss you too. But I want to show you something tonight—something important."

"Show me?" Oliver asked, frowning.

She nodded, her smile widening. "Do you remember A Christmas Carol? The story we used to read together every year?"

He nodded. "You always said it was the perfect Christmas story."

"Well, tonight, we're going to take a little journey. Think of it as your very own Christmas Carol."

"Where are we going?" he asked, his heart pounding with equal parts fear and excitement.

"To the past," she said, standing and offering her hand. "Come on, my dear. There's so much to see."

Before Oliver could ask what she meant, the room began to shift. The walls dissolved into golden light, and the air seemed to hum with energy. He clutched his grandma's hand tightly, his stomach flipping as the light around him grew brighter and brighter. A warmth spread through him, soft and reassuring, like a memory come to life.

When the light faded, he gasped. He wasn't in his room anymore.

3

Christmas Past

The swirling light around them grew brighter, softening into a golden glow that felt both familiar and comforting. When Oliver blinked, he was no longer floating in the haze of the dream but standing in a warm, bustling kitchen. The air was warm and carried a faint, familiar scent that tugged at his memory—it smelled like gingerbread. It took him a moment to realise—it was his grandma's kitchen.

The old oak table was dusted with flour, and the little radio on the windowsill played Christmas carols. The kettle hummed softly on the stove, blending with the cheerful crackle of the fire in the hearth.

"This..." Oliver whispered, turning to his grandma. "This is your house. But how?"

"Do you remember this day?" Grandma asked, smiling as she stepped closer to the table.

Oliver's gaze swept across the room, and his breath caught as he saw his younger self perched on the edge of a chair. The boy was smeared with icing and completely absorbed in decorating the roof of a gingerbread house while Grandma worked beside him, her hands steady and sure.

"I was just thinking about this earlier," Oliver said softly. "I remembered us making that gingerbread house together."

Grandma's smile deepened. "And here it is. Do you see? It wasn't just the gingerbread or the decorations that made Christmas so special—it was the love we poured into everything."

She paused, her gaze steady and kind. "You've always carried Christmas in your heart, Ollie. It's not just the gingerbread or the lights—it's the love we shared that made it magical. That love doesn't disappear, my darling. It changes, like the snow melting into a river. You may not see me the same way, but I'm still here."

Oliver swallowed hard, his voice trembling. "But I can't see you. I can't hear you."

"Not with your eyes or ears, no," Grandma said gently, brushing a strand of hair from his face. "But I'm here in the warmth you feel when you think of me, in the laughter we shared, and in the little things—like when you suddenly remembered this earlier."

She paused, her eyes twinkling. "And do you remember the smell of cinnamon in the kitchen last week, even though no one had been baking? That wasn't just me, Ollie. It's how we—those who love you—find ways to remind you we're near. Sometimes, it's a smell, a song, or just a little tug in your heart—our way of saying, 'We're still with you.'"

He stared at her, memories flickering in his mind. The moments of comfort he couldn't explain, the way this memory had surfaced earlier that evening. "That was you... and Grandad? And...?"

Grandma smiled, her warmth wrapping around him. "All of us, Ollie. We all have ways of reaching out. There will always be ways to feel us close."

Oliver's chest tightened as he watched his younger self carefully place candy canes along the gingerbread roof, completely absorbed in the moment. The scene was so vivid he could almost feel the warmth of the oven and the love that filled the room.

Grandma placed a gentle hand on his shoulder. "Christmas isn't just about what you've lost—it's about what you still have. Open your heart to the love around you, Ollie, and you'll find us in the moments that matter."

The words lingered in the air, wrapping around Oliver like a warm embrace. As he tried to hold onto them, the scene began to shift. The golden light began to swirl around them, gentle at first, then brighter and more vivid. The warmth of the kitchen faded, replaced by the crisp chill of the outdoors. When the light settled, Oliver blinked, finding himself outside in a snowy village.

He recognised it instantly: the high street of their village, decked out in twinkling Christmas lights. Snow drifted softly from the sky, dusting the cobblestones. It was the kind of scene that belonged on a Christmas card.

"I know this day too," Oliver said. He looked around until he spotted them—his younger self, Grandma, and Ben, bundled in scarves and hats, walking toward Miss Sophia's bookshop.

As they pushed open the bookshop's door, a bell tinkled, and the warm light from inside spilled onto the snowy street. Oliver followed them through the door, stepping into a space so familiar it made his chest ache.

Inside, the warmth and smell of spiced biscuits welcomed them. Miss Sophia greeted them with a wide smile, her arms laden with freshly baked gingerbread.

"Now this," Grandma said, nudging the older Oliver, "was one of my favourite traditions. You and

Ben would pick out books, and we'd sit by the fire with hot chocolate."

Oliver watched as the memory unfolded. Ben, barely five years old, held a book almost as big as his head, while Grandma helped him onto a chair. The younger Oliver sat next to them, a steaming mug of hot chocolate in his hands.

"Do you remember how happy you felt here?" Grandma asked. "The warmth, the laughter, the stories? That's Christmas, Ollie. And it doesn't go away just because I'm not here to sit beside you."

Older Oliver swallowed hard. "But it feels... empty without you."

Grandma turned to him, her eyes kind but firm. "Oh, Ollie. I've seen how sad you are and your worries about Christmas never being the same. But you don't need to worry. Even though you can't see me with your eyes, you will always feel me in your heart, enjoying all the Christmas things we did together."

She placed her hand over his chest, and a warmth spread through him. "Every time you bake gingerbread, every time you light the tree, every time you laugh with Ben—I'll be right there with you."

Oliver blinked rapidly, his eyes stinging with tears. "So... you're never really gone?"

Grandma smiled. "Not at all. I'll always be part of the joy you create. And speaking of joy, there's someone else who's been waiting to see you."

Oliver tilted his head, confused. "Who?"

Grandma smiled as if she already knew the answer, gesturing toward the swirling light. "You'll see," she said, stepping back as the light around them began to shift. "Someone else has a gift to share—a way to show you what matters now. But don't worry, Ollie—I'll be close. Always."

As her form began to fade, Oliver felt a wave of warmth and comfort wash over him, as though she'd wrapped him in an invisible hug. The soft glow around him brightened, and he could hear a familiar, booming laugh echoing in the distance.

"Ho, ho, ho!"

The light grew stronger, and Oliver's heart skipped a beat as he realised who it was.

4

Christmas Present

The shimmering light faded, leaving Oliver standing in his own living room. For a moment, he thought he might have woken up, but the scene before him felt... different. Warmer, somehow, like stepping into the glow of a fire after being out in the cold.

And then he saw him—Grandad, sitting comfortably in his favourite armchair, a steaming mug of tea in one hand and a mince pie in the other. His jumper, bright with a Christmas pudding design, stretched slightly over his round belly.

"Grandad?" Oliver whispered, his heart leaping at the sight of him.

"Ho, ho, ho!" Grandad bellowed, his eyes twinkling. "Look at you, lad. Taller than the Christmas tree now, aren't you?"

Oliver felt a smile tug at the corners of his mouth despite himself. "You're... really here?"

"Well, not quite in the flesh," Grandad said, standing and brushing crumbs from his jumper. "But close enough to give you a good talking-to, eh? Now come on, let's have a look at what's what."

Before Oliver could respond, Grandad clapped his hands, and the room seemed to ripple, the furniture melting away like snow under the sun. When the scene re-formed, Oliver realised they were still in the house—but it wasn't quite the same.

In the kitchen, Mum stood at the counter, chopping carrots with slow, deliberate movements. Her face was pale and drawn, and her shoulders sagged as though carrying an invisible weight. She paused for a moment, resting her hands on the counter and looking toward the dining table. It was set with only three plates.

"Your mum's trying so hard, you know," Grandad said gently. "She wants Christmas to be perfect for you and Ben, but it's not easy for her. And more than that, she worries. She worries about you, Ollie. She sees you shut yourself away, and it breaks her heart."

Grandad placed a hand on Oliver's shoulder, his voice soft but steady. "When you think about your mum and feel that little tug in your chest, that's her love reaching out to you, lad. It's how we all communicate, whether we're here or not. Love's like that—it doesn't need words to get through."

He paused, his gaze thoughtful. "And when she looks at you with worry in her eyes, what you feel might be me nudging you too, giving her love a little extra push so it reaches you stronger. We're a team, Ollie. Always have been. So when you feel that spark, don't ignore it—it's us reminding you that you're never alone."

Oliver swallowed hard, the image of his mum standing alone in the kitchen vivid in his mind. The way her shoulders sagged. The way her hands stilled as she looked at the empty chair. He hadn't thought about how much she was carrying on her own.

"She's doing her best, lad," Grandad continued, his voice steady and warm. "You all miss your grandma, but it's not easy for your mum to fill her shoes."

Grandad leaned closer, his tone warm and encouraging. "And here's the thing, Ollie—when you help your mum smile or make Ben laugh, you're not just helping them—you're keeping me alive in those moments too. That's how love works, lad. It's not just about remembering—it's about living with the love we shared and passing it on."

Oliver looked down, guilt swirling in his chest. "I didn't mean to—"

"Don't get stuck in that," Grandad interrupted, his tone kind but firm. "It's not about what you haven't done. It's about what you can still do."

The scene shifted again. This time, Oliver saw his mum and Ben sitting together. Ben's face was lit with excitement as he held up a piece of paper.

"Look, Mum! I made it for Oliver!" Ben said, his voice bright. He held up a hand-drawn card, filled with Christmas trees, stars, and snowflakes. In the corner, a small snowman stood proudly, its rounded body sketched with careful lines. In the centre of the card, Ben had written in large, careful letters: To Oliver, Merry Christmas! I Love You, Ben.

Mum smiled as she reached out to smooth Ben's hair. "He'll love it, sweetheart."

Oliver's chest tightened. He couldn't take his eyes off the card or the joy on Ben's face.

"They're always thinking of you, you know," Grandad said, his voice softer now. "Even when you're shut away in your room. That little brother of yours—he looks up to you more than you realise."

Grandad gestured toward the snowman on the card, his eyes twinkling. "Look there, lad—see the snowman Ben drew in the corner? That's no coincidence. It's just like the snowman ornament you made with your grandma when you were small. Sometimes, we guide others in ways you might not even notice. That's us saying, 'We're still here, cheering you on.'"

Oliver's voice trembled as he whispered, "You mean... you and Grandma?"

Grandad smiled warmly. "Aye, and others too. Love doesn't stop, Ollie—it just finds new ways to reach you. That snowman? That's a little reminder that we're never far."

Oliver swallowed hard, his throat tight with emotion. "But I... I've been so distant."

The air around them shimmered again, and before Oliver could say more, the scene began to change. The warm glow of the house gave way to a crisp, snowy landscape. They stood now by the village green, which was blanketed in fresh snow. The twinkling Christmas lights from the lampposts cast a soft glow on the scene.

Nearby, a group of children were rolling enormous snowballs, laughing and shouting as they worked together to build a snowman. Oliver squinted and recognised them immediately—they were his friends.

"Look at them," Grandad said, gesturing toward the children.

Oliver's chest tightened as he saw one of his friends pause, brushing snow off his gloves. "I wonder how Oliver's doing," the boy said. "He would've loved this."

Another friend, who was helping to lift a snowball into place, nodded solemnly. "Yeah. He hasn't wanted to do anything for weeks. He's such a good friend... I just wish we could do something to help him."

Oliver's stomach churned. He stepped forward, wanting to call out, to tell them he was fine, but his voice wouldn't come.

"Do you see, lad?" Grandad said gently, his tone carrying a mix of encouragement and urgency. "You're missing all this, and they miss you too. It's not just your mum and Ben. Your friends care about you too. They want you to be happy. But you've got to let them in."

Oliver's eyes stayed fixed on the scene before him. Every year, they'd built snowmen together, laughing until their cheeks ached from the cold. He hadn't realised how much he missed those moments. The memories surged within him, filling his chest with a bittersweet ache.

"I... I didn't realise," Oliver whispered, watching as his friends burst into laughter, one of them slipping and landing in the snow.

Grandad placed a firm but gentle hand on his shoulder, his voice warm and steady. "Your grandma and I always knew it, lad. It's in the way you light up a room, just like her. You've got it in you—you always have."

Oliver swallowed hard, the lump in his throat making it difficult to speak. "But what if I've forgotten how?" he asked, his voice barely above a whisper.

Grandad smiled warmly, his grip steady on Oliver's shoulder. "You've got a good heart, lad. Just follow it. Bring joy to others, and you'll find it'll bring you joy in return. You've got so much love to give, Ollie. Don't let it go to waste."

The snowy scene shimmered and began to fade, leaving Oliver with the echoes of his friends' laughter and Grandad's reassuring words.

The light around them softened, returning them to the warmth of the living room. Oliver found himself standing once more amidst the familiar sights and sounds of home—Ben's laughter echoing faintly downstairs, the gentle hum of the house.

Grandad turned to him, his expression kind but resolute. "That's why I'm here," he said, resting a steady hand on Oliver's shoulder once again. "To remind you that Christmas isn't just about what we've lost—it's about what we still have. Your family and your friends need you, Ollie. They love you."

The weight of it all settled heavily on Oliver's chest. "What am I supposed to do?" he whispered. "I can't bring Grandma back. I can't make it like it used to be."

"No, you can't," Grandad said gently. "But you can make it something new. Something just as special. It's not about what's missing, Ollie—it's about what you bring to the table. Whether it's laughter with Ben or helping your mum bake gingerbread again. Those little things? They make all the difference."

Oliver thought back to the vision of his friends building their snowman, their laughter still echoing in his ears. He thought of Ben and Mum, waiting downstairs. His heart ached.

"What if I can't?" he asked, his voice small but steady.

Grandad's booming laugh filled the room, a sound so full of warmth it seemed to chase away the shadows. "Oh, nonsense! You've got more love in you than you know, lad. You just need to use it. Start small—go downstairs. Play with Ben. Give your mum a hand. And your friends? Let them know you're still here. You'll be amazed at what a little kindness can do."

Oliver hesitated, the idea both comforting and daunting. "Is it too late?"

"Too late?" Grandad grinned, patting Oliver on the shoulder. "It's Christmas, lad. If there's one thing the season teaches us—aside from the importance of love and kindness—it's that Christmas is a time when the most magical things can happen."

Grandad's voice softened, his eyes shining. "You've got a good heart, Ollie. Follow it. Bring joy to others, and you'll see how much it brings back to you. That's what Christmas is all about and that's what your grandma always knew.

Before Oliver could respond, the scene began to shift. The light around them grew brighter, soft and golden, as the edges of the room dissolved. Grandad stepped back, his form starting to fade, but his voice stayed steady, filled with warmth.

"I'll leave you with that, lad," Grandad said, his voice warm and steady. "But you're not done yet. There's someone else who's been waiting a long time to see you. Be ready, Ollie. What they'll show you might just change everything."

The glow engulfed Oliver, and as the last traces of Grandad's laugh faded, the faint scent of tea and mince pies lingered in the air, a reminder of the love that would always guide him.

5

Christmas Yet to Come

The golden light around Oliver softened, turning into a radiant, silvery glow that filled the space with a quiet stillness. The air seemed to hum gently, as if waiting for something wonderful to unfold. Oliver's heart began beating faster with a mix of anticipation and awe.

From the silvery haze, a figure began to emerge. At first, it was no more than a shadow, but as the light grew stronger, Oliver felt something deep within him—a warmth, a recognition beyond memory. His heart swelled, almost as if it knew before his mind could catch up.

The figure stepped closer, and suddenly, Oliver knew.

"Dad?" he whispered, his voice barely audible. The word carried all the wonder, disbelief, and longing that had been locked in his heart for years.

The man smiled, his eyes warm and filled with love. He was exactly as Oliver had seen him in photographs—tall, with kind eyes and a gentle strength. But there was something more: an energy that radiated through the air, filling the room with peace and love.

"Yes, son," his father said, his voice calm and steady. "It's me."

A rush of loving energy filled Oliver, as if the warmth and light in the room had entered his very being. Before he could think, he ran forward. His father opened his arms, and they embraced tightly. It was as if all the years of separation melted away in that single moment.

Oliver felt his father's love wrap around him like a warm blanket, and tears streamed down his face.

"I've missed you so much," Oliver said, his voice trembling.

"And I've never been far, Ollie," his dad said gently, resting a hand on Oliver's back. "I've been with you every step of the way. I've watched you grow, watched you become the wonderful boy you are today. I've even been there when you played football, cheering you on. And I'm so proud of you."

Oliver stepped back slightly, looking up into his father's face. "You've been here? Really?"

His dad nodded. "Always. You might not have seen me, but I've been with you—in your thoughts, in your heart, in the love you've shared with others.

Oliver felt a warmth bloom in his chest at the thought. He looked up at his dad, his heart swelling with so many questions he didn't know where to begin. What had his dad been doing all this time? Was he happy? What was it like where he was? But more than anything, Oliver just wanted to stay here with him, to hold onto this moment. It felt right and so good to be near him again, as if a missing piece had finally fallen into place.

His father's gaze was soft, as though he could see every question swirling in Oliver's mind. "It's difficult to explain in physical terms because time and space work differently here. Where I am is peaceful and full of love—there's no pain, no sadness, just... the quiet knowing that everything is as it should be. But, Ollie, I'm also able to see you, to be near you. I've seen your days, your moments of joy, your struggles. I'm not gone, Ollie. I've just changed. I'm like the wind brushing past you, the robin that lands in your garden, the whisper of a thought when you need it most. I'm here in ways you can feel, even if you can't see me."

Oliver nodded, though he still couldn't fully grasp it. He hesitated, his voice small but trembling with longing. "How long are you staying?"

The warmth in Oliver's chest faltered, and the sharp pang of sadness at losing his dad all over again felt unbearable. "I've only just met you," he whispered, his voice cracking.

His father reached out, placing a hand over Oliver's heart. The touch sent a wave of the most profound warmth and joy through Oliver's body. It was as if all the sadness, all the heaviness in his chest, melted away, replaced by a glowing sense of love and peace.

His father spoke with quiet reassurance, his voice calm and steady. "Ollie, I wish I could stay with you here, just like this, but that's not the way it works. Even if I could stay longer, the time would still come when it was time to go. What's more important is for you to understand that I've never really left you—and I never will. I've been with you all along, just as your grandma and grandad have. We'll always be close, even if you can't see us as you have tonight."

Oliver looked up into his father's kind eyes, feeling the weight and truth of his words settle deep in his heart.

"But how will I feel it?" Oliver asked quietly, his voice trembling just a little.

Sometimes, it's a feeling you can't explain or a sudden memory. And other times," he added gently, "you might see something—a little sign—to remind you we're near."

His father smiled, the corners of his eyes crinkling with affection. "Sometimes, it's a it's a sudden feeling or a memory. And other times," his father added gently, "it might be something that feels like a coincidence—like hearing our song on the radio just at the right time, or finding an old photo you didn't even know you'd kept. Those aren't accidents, Ollie. They're our way of reminding you we're here."

Oliver frowned slightly, his brow furrowing. "I'm still not sure I understand."

His dad's smile deepened, as though he'd been expecting this. "Alright then, let me give you an example." He paused, his voice warm and playful now. "Have you ever wondered why that robin always shows up in the garden at Christmas?"

Oliver blinked. "The robin? Yes, it comes every year. Every time I see it, I feel so good."

His father's expression glowed with quiet affection. "That's me, Ollie. That little robin is my way of saying hello and bringing you a little bit of joy."

Oliver swallowed the lump rising in his throat. The sadness he'd felt earlier was still there, but it no longer weighed him down. Instead, it was wrapped in love, hope, and the quiet certainty that his dad, his grandma, and his grandad were never truly gone.

Tears filled Oliver's eyes and spilled freely down his cheeks, but they weren't tears of sorrow. They carried something brighter—something full of love and promise. "I'll remember," he whispered. "I'll remember all of you. And I'll try to make Christmas special again. For Mum and Ben. For everyone."

His father smiled, pride shining in his eyes. "That's all we've ever wanted for you, Ollie. To be happy, to love, and to share that love with others. When you wake, remember this: we're always with you, and you have so much happiness to look forward to in all your future Christmases. And when you forget, I'll send you a robin to remind you."

Oliver nodded, his heart full. He opened his mouth to say more, but the light around his father began to dim, softening until it was no more than a gentle glow. Even as his figure faded into the distance, the love he left behind stayed, wrapping Oliver in a tender embrace.

6

Waking Up to Joy

The house was quiet, cloaked in the lingering darkness of a winter morning. Outside, the world lay hushed beneath its snowy blanket, the cold pressing gently against the windows.

Oliver stirred, his eyes fluttering open briefly. The air around him was cool, but his bed was a sanctuary of warmth and comfort. He rolled over, ready to let the cosiness pull him back to sleep.

But then it hit him—like a wave of light and love.

The dream.

"It all rushed back at once: Grandma's kind smile, Grandad's hearty laugh, and the glowing embrace of his dad. Every word, every moment was so vivid it felt as though they were still with him. His heart swelled, not with sadness but with joy—a joy so full and radiant it made him want to leap out of bed."

"Oliver sat up, clutching the snowman ornament he'd fallen asleep holding. He couldn't stop smiling.

As the warmth of his dream lingered, other memories surfaced—the sadness on his mum's face, weighed down by her worries and the effort of holding everything together. And Ben... Ben excitedly asking him to watch a movie, only to be met with silence. The sound of his brother's rejected footsteps still echoed painfully in his heart.

He'd shut them out, locked himself away, and now he realised just how much he'd missed.

Suddenly, it dawned on him—something so wonderful. Oliver's eyes widened, and his smile grew brighter. "It's Christmas Eve," he whispered, his voice tinged with wonder. "It's not too late."

It wasn't too late to play with Ben, to bring him the joy he'd seen in his dream. It wasn't too late to ease his mum's worries, to show her she didn't have to carry it all on her own. He had the whole day ahead—a chance to bring to life the love and light that still glowed in his chest.

Throwing back the covers, Oliver jumped out of bed and dashed into the hallway. He tiptoed into his mum's room and found her still curled up beneath the duvet.

"Mum," Oliver said softly, leaning down to kiss her cheek. "Happy Christmas Eve. I love you."

His mum stirred, blinking up at him in surprise. "Oliver?" she murmured, sitting up. "What's this about?"

He grinned, wrapping her in a hug. "I just wanted to say it. I love you."

Without waiting for a reply, he dashed out of the room and into Ben's, bursting through the door. Ben was snuggled under his blanket, clutching a stuffed reindeer. Oliver knelt by his bed and shook his shoulder gently.

"Ben! Wake up! It's Christmas Eve!"

Ben's eyes opened groggily, and he frowned. "What are you doing? You never wake me up."

Oliver laughed and pulled him into a hug, squishing him against his chest. "I know. But today's different. Come on, sleepyhead. Do you want to play?"

Ben's face lit up as he wriggled free. "Really? You mean it?"

"Of course I mean it!" Oliver said, ruffling his hair. "Come on."

At breakfast, the house buzzed with a warmth that hadn't been there for months. Oliver's mum watched in astonishment as her eldest son chatted and laughed with Ben, his enthusiasm infectious.

Between bites of toast, Oliver tried to explain his dream. "It was incredible," he said, gesturing wildly with his hands. "Grandma, Grandad, even Dad—they were all there. And they told me... they told me they're always with us. Not in a sad way, but in a way that makes everything better."

"His mum's eyes glistened as she reached across the table to squeeze his hand. 'Ollie, that's... incredible,' she said, her voice filled with wonder. 'What an amazing gift to feel them so close again.'"

Ben's eyes widened, his fork hovering mid-air. "You saw Dad and Grandma and Grandad? Really?" His voice was high-pitched with excitement.

Oliver nodded, his grin widening. "Really, Ben. It felt so real—like they were right here with me."

Ben bounced slightly in his seat, nearly upsetting his glass of orange juice. "What did they say? Did they talk about me?"

Oliver chuckled. "Of course they did. They're always thinking about you, Ben. They're so proud of you too."

Ben's face lit up with pure joy. "I wish I could have a dream like that. Maybe tonight! Do you think they'd visit me too?"

His mum reached over to ruffle Ben's hair. "You never know, sweetheart. Miracles can happen, especially at Christmas."

Ben beamed at the thought, his cheeks glowing pink. Then, suddenly, his attention snapped back to Oliver. "Does this mean you'll play with me today? Maybe they told you to!"

Oliver laughed. "Alright, alright. You've convinced me. Let's play after breakfast—just don't expect me to go easy on you!"

Ben cheered, his excitement infectious, and the warmth around the table grew even brighter.

The day unfolded like a dream of its own. Oliver helped his mum tidy up the living room, laughing as they raced to see who could collect the most Christmas decorations from the floor. When Ben suggested watching a Christmas movie, Oliver didn't hesitate to grab the remote and sit beside him on the couch.

But the best part of the morning came when Oliver had an idea. "Mum," he said, "do you think we could go to Miss Sophia's bookshop? You know, like we used to. Hot chocolate, gingerbread, the works."

His mum's face softened, and for the first time in weeks, her smile reached her eyes. "I think that's a lovely idea."

7

Miss Sophia's Bookshop

After lunch, the three of them bundled up in scarves and coats and set off for the village. The streets were dusted with snow, and at times the air carried the faint scent of woodsmoke and pine. Oliver felt lighter with every step, the warmth of the morning still glowing in his chest.

They strolled past shop windows adorned with bright festive displays until they reached the familiar painted sign of Miss Sophia's bookshop. Oliver stopped for a moment, taking it in. The window glowed softly, framed by strands of evergreen garlands and twinkling lights.

"Come on!" Ben said, tugging at Oliver's hand. His younger brother was practically bouncing with excitement.

The bell above the door chimed as they stepped inside, and a wave of warmth and nostalgia washed over Oliver. The sweet, comforting scent of hot chocolate hit him first, followed by the delicate, refreshing aroma of mint tea. It felt like stepping into a world where Christmas lived and breathed.

Shelves overflowed with books, their spines catching the soft, golden glow of fairy lights woven delicately among them. A fir tree stood in the corner, its branches adorned with ornaments shaped like stars, snowflakes, and tiny books. Their favourite table by the bay window awaited them, offering the cozy warmth of the fire and a view of the snow-dusted high street outside.

Miss Sophia appeared almost instantly, her face lighting up when she saw them. She was a vision of warmth, her rosy cheeks framed by her silvery hair. For a fleeting moment, as she took in the sight of the family stepping into her shop, she was half expecting to see their grandma, her oldest friend, walk through the door. The realization hit her in an instant: their grandma wouldn't be with them this year. A bittersweet pang stirred in her chest, but it was quickly replaced by a wave of affection for the family.

"Well, if it isn't my favorite family!" she said, hurrying over to greet them. She pulled their mum into a warm hug, her eyes glistening with affection. "How are you, my dear?"

Their mum smiled, though her voice wavered with emotion. "I'm well, Miss Sophia. I've missed coming here."

Miss Sophia turned her gaze to Oliver and Ben, her expression softening further. "And how about you two? Are you ready for your usual Christmas treat?"

The boys nodded eagerly, their faces lighting up. Oliver couldn't help but smile. There was something about Miss Sophia's presence that reminded him of

Grandma—a kindness and understanding that seemed to fill the entire shop.

As she showed them to their table, Oliver felt a familiar glow spread through him. It was as if Grandma herself were standing beside him, her love reaching out through the cozy shop. Tears prickled at the corners of his eyes, and he turned toward the window to collect himself.

Their hot chocolates arrived shortly after, crowned with whipped cream, sprinkles, and tiny candy canes perched on the rims. The boys sipped eagerly, the warmth spreading through them like a hug.

As their mum excused herself to browse the shelves, Oliver leaned toward Ben. "Do you think Miss Sophia has any family?" he asked, his voice quiet.

Ben frowned slightly. "I don't know," he said, glancing toward Miss Sophia, who was tidying a stack of books. "Why?"

Oliver hesitated, his gaze following Ben's. "I just think... she shouldn't be alone at Christmas."

When their mum returned moments later, her arms filled with books, Oliver shared his thoughts. Her expression softened, and she glanced toward Miss Sophia, her smile tinged with quiet understanding. "She doesn't have family nearby," she said gently. "That's such a thoughtful idea, Ollie."

"Do you think we could invite her?" Oliver asked, his voice brightening.

"I think she'd love that," their mum said. "Would you boys like to invite her yourselves?"

They didn't need to be asked twice. The boys leapt from their seats and hurried over to the counter. Miss Sophia turned, her smile widening when she saw them approach.

"Miss Sophia," Oliver began, his voice steady but warm, "we were wondering—would you like to have Christmas dinner with us tomorrow?"

Ben chimed in, his words tumbling over each other. "Mum says you don't have anyone close by, and we'd really love to have you. Please say yes!"

For a moment, Miss Sophia seemed taken aback. She looked at the two boys, her eyes glistening with unspoken emotion. She placed a hand on her chest, as if to steady herself. "Oh, my dears," she said softly, her voice trembling. "That's the kindest thing anyone has offered me in years."

Oliver and Ben beamed, and she reached out, pulling them both into a gentle hug. "I would love to join you," she said, her voice thick with gratitude. "On one condition."

"What's that?" Ben asked, his eyes wide.

"I'll bring along some of my famous Christmas cookies," she said with a playful wink

The boys laughed and hugged her again, then dashed back to the table to share the wonderful news with their mum.

As Oliver sat down, he couldn't help but feel the same glowing warmth from his dream, as if Grandma herself were smiling down on them.

8

'Twas the Night Before Christmas

T he walk home from the village was magical. Snowflakes drifted lazily through the crisp evening air, and the glow of the streetlamps lit their path. Ben ran ahead, his scarf trailing behind him, while Oliver and their mum followed behind, chatting and enjoying the moment. Oliver couldn't stop smiling; the warmth of Miss Sophia's bookshop and the joy of the day lingered in his chest, like a glowing ember he never wanted to lose.

By the time they reached home, the windows were frosted with the cold outside, but the house itself was a haven of warmth and comfort. They hung up their coats and scarves, kicked off their boots, and lingered by the fire to warm their hands. Mum disappeared into the kitchen to prepare dinner.

"Come on, Ben," Oliver said, coaxing his little brother into a game to keep him entertained while they waited. They played by the fire, their laughter filling the room, and for a moment, Oliver forgot about everything else—he was just happy.

It was going to be Ben's favourite—her homemade soup and chunks of fresh bread they had bought from the bakery in the village earlier. Ben chattered away as he dipped his bread in his soup, his excitement bubbling over as he recounted every detail of their visit to the village and Miss Sophia's shop. Their mum smiled, joining in the conversation, and Oliver couldn't help but notice how much lighter she seemed tonight.

In the quiet of the moment, Oliver's thoughts drifted to his dream, where he had seen his mum in the kitchen, her face etched with a quiet sadness and worry as she tried so hard to make Christmas special for him and Ben.

He looked down at his soup, appreciating the comforting warmth of the meal and the care it symbolized. "Thanks for dinner, Mum," he said, looking up with a smile. "It is lovely."

Her eyes softened, and she reached over to squeeze his hand. "I'm glad you like it, Ollie."

Oliver helped his mum tidy up, a smile spreading across his face as he watched Ben copy him, carefully carrying his plate into the kitchen before settling on the sofa. Soon, they all gathered for a Christmas movie. Ben curled up under a blanket between Oliver and their mum, and Oliver couldn't help but marvel at how right everything felt. As the movie played, he and Ben laughed together at the antics on screen, their voices blending with the gentle crackle of the fire.

This is what Grandad meant, Oliver thought, his heart swelling. Christmas could still be good—different, yes, but good. The warmth of the moment wrapped around him, as comforting as the blanket Ben had pulled over himself.

When the movie ended, the room felt hushed and peaceful, the kind of quiet that only Christmas evenings seemed to bring. Ben let out a big yawn, his eyes drooping even as he tried to stay awake. Their mum ruffled his hair gently and coaxed him upstairs, despite his sleepy murmurs of, "Just five more minutes..."

Oliver stayed up a little longer, helping his mum tidy up. She gave him a soft smile as he straightened the cushions on the sofa. "It's been a good day, hasn't it?" she said.

"The best," Oliver replied, and as he made his way upstairs, he couldn't shake the feeling that Christmas was truly beginning to feel magical again.

As he lay in bed, his thoughts returned to the dream that had changed everything. He closed his eyes and let the memories wash over him—the golden glow, Grandma's smile, Grandad's booming laugh, and his dad's gentle presence. It all felt so real, so close, as if they were right there with him.

His mind drifted back to the wonderful visit to Miss Sophia's bookshop. There had been something about Miss Sophia —her presence had felt warm and familiar. Sitting there in the cosy shop, it had felt almost as though Grandma was with him.

He whispered into the stillness, "Grandma, I'm sure you were there. Were you?"

There was no reply, but the warmth in his chest deepened, and he smiled, a quiet certainty settling over him. Maybe it didn't matter if he could hear her answer—he could feel it.

Turning his thoughts to Grandad, he said, "You were right, Grandad. Christmas can be good again, even though it's different. Thank you for showing me."

Finally, he whispered to his dad, "I'll be looking for the robin tomorrow, Dad. I hope I'll feel you near."

The fullness of the day, the love in his heart, and the quiet peace of Christmas Eve wrapped around him like a soft blanket. He drifted into a deep, contented sleep.

9

A Christmas Miracle

The next morning, Oliver awoke feeling wonderful. For a moment, he lay still, savouring the lingering sense of warmth and happiness from the night before. Then, in an instant, it hit him—it was Christmas Day!

He threw back the covers and sprang out of bed, his heart racing with excitement. He hurried into his mum's room, just as he had the day before, and leaned down to kiss her cheek.

"Happy Christmas, Mum!" he said brightly. "I love you."

His mum opened her eyes and smiled. "Merry Christmas, Ollie," she said, her voice warm with affection.

Oliver didn't linger long. He darted to Ben's room, throwing open the door. "Ben! It's Christmas! Come on, get up!"

Ben sat up, his hair sticking up in every direction, and grinned. "It's Christmas!" he shouted, scrambling out of bed.

The morning unfolded like a dream. They gathered around the tree, its lights sparkling like tiny stars, and began opening their gifts. The room was filled with delighted laughter, the crinkle of wrapping paper and heartfelt thank-yous.

Oliver watched his brother's face light up with pure joy as he examined each new treasure, and his mum smiled with a warmth that filled his heart with happiness.

This, Oliver thought, *is Christmas.*

After the initial excitement—the flurry of laughter and excitement as they shared their surprises—the house began to settle into a calm rhythm. Their mum had gone into the kitchen to continue all her Christmas preparations, leaving Oliver and Ben to their game.

For a while, the only sounds were the soft clatter of game pieces and the occasional crackle from the fireplace. But as the stillness settled around him, Oliver's thoughts began to wander, drawn to the empty chair by the fire.

It was in that quiet moment that Oliver felt it—the weight of her absence. His gaze drifted to the empty armchair by the fire, the one where his grandma would always sit on Christmas Day. She'd have her knitting in her lap, a mug of tea on the table beside her, and a warm smile for everyone in the room. The sight was so vivid in his mind that it almost felt real, and yet the emptiness of the chair made it all the more clear that she wasn't there.

The sadness crept in, soft but steady, wrapping around him like a familiar, unwelcome visitor. It lingered, pressing against his chest as he whispered under his breath, "I miss you, Grandma."

The words hung in the stillness for a moment. But as the sadness deepened, the memory of his dream stirred within him. He remembered the golden glow, the warmth, and the love that had enveloped him. He remembered her words—the reassurance that the love they shared was still with him, always.

His eyes fell back on Ben, who was frowning in concentration as he lined up his next move on the board. Without a word, Oliver leaned over and wrapped his arms around him in a tight hug.

Ben looked up, startled. "What's this for?"

"This is a great Christmas, isn't it?" Oliver said, his voice steady but warm.

Ben's face lit up with a wide grin. "The best!" he said, hugging Oliver back fiercely.

As they finished their game, Oliver stood and stretched. "I'm just going to see if Mum needs any help," he said, ruffling Ben's hair as he headed toward the kitchen.

There, his mum stood at the counter, peeling potatoes. She turned to him with a soft smile.

"Everything alright, Ollie?"

Oliver nodded, his chest swelling with gratitude. "It's a great day, Mum. Thank you for everything you've done."

His mum's eyes glistened as she set down the peeler. "That means the world to me, love."

"And," Oliver added, grinning, "what can I do to help?"

His mum laughed, wiping her hands on her apron. "You offering to help with dinner? Now that's a Christmas miracle!"

10

A Sign of Love

The sound of the doorbell rang out just as Oliver reached for the peeler.

"That'll be Miss Sophia," his mum said, her face lighting up.

Before Oliver could respond, Ben came rushing in from the living room, his face alight with excitement. "It's Miss Sophia! She's here!"

The feeling of warmth that Oliver had experienced in the bookshop the day before returned, wrapping around him like a gentle hug as they all went to the door.

When they opened it, Miss Sophia stood there, beaming. Snowflakes clung to her hair and the shoulders of her coat. In one hand, she held a large bag bulging with Christmas gifts, and tucked under her other arm was a package wrapped in the unmistakable brown paper of her bookshop.

"I hope you're in the mood for some Christmas cookies," she said, handing the brown paper parcel to Ben and Oliver with a wink.

"Merry Christmas!" she added, stepping inside and shaking the snow from her coat.

Miss Sophia wasn't like any usual guest. As she hung up her coat, Oliver noticed she was wearing her favourite apron underneath. She smiled and said, "I'm more comfortable helping in the kitchen. What can I do?"

His mum laughed warmly. "Come on, then. Let's get you busy."

Miss Sophia followed her into the kitchen, rolling up her sleeves with a playful determination. "It smells wonderful in here already," she said, glancing around at the bubbling pots and neatly prepared vegetables.

Oliver lingered for a moment in the doorway to the kitchen, watching as the two women fell into an easy rhythm—chopping, stirring, and laughing together. It reminded him of how his mum and Grandma used to cook together—different, yes, but just as warm and comforting.

Ben had settled by the Christmas tree, holding one of Miss Sophia's large Christmas tree cookies in his hand, nibbling at the edges as he admired his new toys.

Oliver sat next to him, helping him learn how to use his new remote-controlled car, their laughter mingling with the crackle of the fire.

After finishing all the preparations for Christmas dinner, Mum and Miss Sophia came into the living room to relax with a cup of tea. They settled on the sofa, watching the boys play.

"Oh, I almost forgot," Miss Sophia said suddenly, reaching into her bag. She pulled out a neatly wrapped package, holding it up with a smile. "I've brought homemade Christmas pudding for dessert. Does anyone here like Christmas pudding?"

"I do!" Oliver said eagerly. And as the words left his mouth, he could have sworn he heard Grandad's voice in the back of his mind, booming with laughter: "I do too!" Or perhaps it wasn't a voice—just a feeling, strong and certain.

Dinner was perfect. The table was surrounded by laughter and love, the pulling of Christmas crackers, and the telling of jokes from the crackers that would have made Grandad proud.

Oliver felt a wave of appreciation as he looked around the room. His mum, smiling brighter than she had in months. Ben giggling as he tried to hide his Brussels sprouts under some mashed potato. And Miss Sophia, her laughter mingling with his mum's, the two of them sharing a warmth that made the house feel even more alive. Seeing them so happy filled Oliver with a quiet joy of his own.

As he took it all in, Oliver couldn't help but think of his grandma. The arrival of Miss Sophia carried the same kind of warmth his grandma always brought to Christmas, and the Christmas pudding on the table, paired with the silly cracker jokes, made him think of Grandad. Yet, even with the joy filling the room, a part of him still longed to feel his dad's presence, just as his dad had promised in his dream.

Just as the thought crossed his mind, there was a knock at the door.

He frowned. A visitor on Christmas Day? That was unusual. He opened the door and found five of his friends standing there, their cheeks pink from the cold and their eyes gleaming with mischief.

Merry Christmas!" they shouted in unison, their cheeks flushed from the cold. Before Oliver could respond, they launched into a cheerful carol, their voices spilling into laughter halfway through the first verse

Oliver stared at them in astonishment, his mouth open in surprise. Then, as their laughter grew, a grin broke across his face, and he couldn't help but join in. "What are you all doing here?" he asked, his voice bubbling with laughter.

One of his friends shrugged. "We thought we'd visit. We didn't want you to feel alone—we figured this Christmas might be a bit quiet for you, so we thought we'd liven it up!"

"Come in," Oliver said, his grin widening. "You have to meet Miss Sophia—she brought her Christmas cookies—they're amazing!"

The house became alive with joy. Oliver's friends had gathered around the tree, their laughter filling the room, while Ben was doubled over, giggling uncontrollably at something one of them had said. From the kitchen came the sound of his mum and Miss Sophia chatting happily, like old friends.

Oliver paused, letting the warmth of it all sink in. He couldn't remember a Christmas as good as this.

As soon as the thought passed through his mind, a feeling of guilt washed over him, sharp and unexpected. How could he think that when his grandma wasn't here? She had done so much to make Christmases magical for all of them, year after year.

But before the feeling could take hold, something stirred deep within him—that warm, glowing love from his dream. He remembered his grandma's words, her reassurance that the love they shared would always be with him. In an instant, he knew: his grandma wouldn't want him to feel guilty for enjoying Christmas. She would want him to be happy, to embrace the joy and love that surrounded him.

As the guilt melted away, Oliver caught a movement in the corner of his eye. He turned to the window just in time to see a robin flutter down and land on the glistening ice of the windowsill.

The robin was so small and perfect, its bright red chest glowing like a tiny ember against the frosty glass, warming his heart. It tilted its head, hopping closer until it was no more than a few feet away.

Oliver was transfixed, fully absorbed in the moment. It was as if the robin looked directly at him, its dark eyes filled with a quiet knowing.

In the stillness, he felt it—the presence of his dad, just as he had in his dream. Tears welled up in Oliver's eyes, not from sadness but from a profound sense of love and connection.

Then with a flutter of its wings, the robin took off, just as quickly as it had arrived, disappearing into the snowy sky.

Oliver smiled to himself, the tears still glistening in his eyes. He knew that the robin's visit was no coincidence. It was the sign he had hoped for—the sign that his dad was near, just as he had promised in his dream.

11

The Greatest Gift

After the robin's visit, the garden beyond the frosted glass seemed even more still and quiet, the snow glistening faintly under the soft glow spilling from the living room. Oliver stood by the window, his gaze fixed on the wintry scene outside. A gentle sense of peace settled over him as he thought about everything that had happened—the dream, the robin, and the warmth that filled his heart now.

Behind him, the room brimmed with laughter and chatter. He could hear Ben's giggles and the playful banter of his friends, a comforting backdrop to his thoughts. For a moment, Oliver simply stood there, appreciating the joy and light that seemed to fill every corner of the house.

"Hey, Oliver," a quiet voice said behind him, breaking through his reverie.

Oliver turned to see Peter standing nearby, his hands deep in his pockets. There was a hesitancy in Peter's expression, but also something earnest and thoughtful.

"It's so good to see you smiling and enjoying Christmas," Peter began. "I've seen how hard it's been for you. But now... you seem to have found some happiness. And I'm really happy for you, mate. I just..." He trailed off, staring at the floor.

"What is it?" Oliver prompted gently.

Peter looked up, his eyes shadowed with emotion. "I don't know if I'll ever feel that way. I still have moments—almost every day—when I feel sad about my mum. Even after two years, it can still feel so hard sometimes. I don't know how to make it better"

Oliver's heart ached for his friend. "You're right," Oliver said softly. "I was so sad. And I still am sometimes. But then something happened that changed how I think about it." He paused, searching for the right words. "I had this dream... it might sound strange, but it felt so real. I felt the presence of my grandma and my grandad too. They helped me see that they're still with me, in a way. I can't see them or hear them, but I can feel them."

Peter frowned slightly, trying to process Oliver's words. "Feel them? How?"

Oliver smiled faintly. "Sometimes, I notice things that remind me of my grandma—like gingerbread or knitting. It's like I feel closer to her through them. When I feel love for her, it feels like... I can feel her love for me too, like we're sharing it. And now I'm starting to think, maybe she even guides me toward those things so we can have that connection."

Peter tilted his head, considering this.

"No one can prove it isn't real," Oliver added firmly. "Some might say it's just my imagination, but for me, it feels real."

Peter nodded slowly, his expression thoughtful. "You know," he began, "something happened earlier that feels different now after listening to you." He hesitated, glancing at Oliver. "When the others said they wanted to come visit you, I wasn't sure about leaving home. I thought I should stay with my dad and my sister—be there for them. But then my dad said, 'Your mum would want you to go and have some time with your friends.'"

Oliver raised his eyebrows slightly, sensing something important in Peter's tone.

"At the time, I thought it was just my dad trying to make it easier for me to go," Peter continued, "but now... now I'm not so sure. Being here with everyone—it's so nice. Like amazing! And now, talking with you—I feel like she really did want me to come. Like she was guiding me here."

Peter paused, his voice quiet but full of gratitude. "What you said... it makes me think differently about her. Like maybe she's still guiding me even now. Thanks for that. It really helps."

Oliver smiled, warmth spreading through him. "I'm glad, Peter. I really am."

As Oliver spoke, Peter's gaze drifted to the window. The tiny robin had returned, perched delicately on the icy sill. Its red chest stood out proudly, as if the little bird had come not only to share its beauty but also to bring something special.

Peter was captivated, his gaze fixed on the robin as it sat there, small and perfect. Then, with a gentle flutter of its wings, the robin lifted off into the snowy night. In its wake, something else floated gently down—a small feather, resting softly on the windowsill, caught in the golden light spilling from the living room.

Peter's breath caught for a moment.

"A feather," he murmured, his voice barely above a whisper.

Oliver followed Peter's gaze and his eyes landed on the delicate feather resting softly against the frosty glass. "Does it mean something to you?" he asked gently.

Peter nodded slowly, his eyes glistening. "My mum... she always said that feathers were a sign from loved ones. Whenever she found one, she said she felt it was a sign from her own grandma. I used to think it was just something she said to comfort herself, but now..."

Peter trailed off, his gaze locked on the feather. He let out a soft, tearful laugh. "Now I'm not so sure."

Oliver's smile deepened, filled with warmth. "Maybe that feather was just for you."

Peter turned to him, his expression a mix of wonder and gratitude. "Maybe it was."

As their attention returned to the room, laughter and chatter embraced them once again. Oliver's eyes swept across the room, taking in the scene—the people he loved, the happiness that filled the space. Then his attention was drawn to the mantel above the fire, where three Christmas cards sat side by side. One featured a Christmas pudding, another a snowman, and the last, a robin.

Oliver stared at the cards, their simple images speaking volumes to his heart. His grandad, his grandma, his dad—there they were. The warmth he'd felt in his dream stirred within him again, steady and certain. They would never truly be far away.

A gentle smile spread across his face as he turned back to the room. Ben caught his eye and waved him over to join the game by the tree, his giggles spilling into the room like music. Miss Sophia and his mum were at the table, their joy adding to the love that filled the room. Peter looked at him with quiet gratitude, his smile soft and full of understanding.

With his heart overflowing, Oliver glanced at his grandma's empty armchair by the fire. To his delight, he didn't feel sadness this time. Instead, a warm memory filled him—the two of them together by the fire, her voice lively and full of love as she read *A Christmas Carol*.

The memory filled him with a gentle warmth, bringing not loss, but joy. As he relived it, he turned toward his friends and family, his gaze sweeping over the faces of the people he loved. Each one filled his heart with gratitude.

Tiny Tim's heartfelt words echoed in his mind, and with a spark of inspiration, he said, "Hey, everyone!"

The chatter quieted as they all turned to face him. Smiling deeply, his voice strong and full of warmth, Oliver spoke Tiny Tim's words:

"A Merry Christmas to us all; God bless us, everyone!"

The room erupted in laughter and cheers, Ben clapping his hands excitedly, as love and happiness swirled through the house.

And in that moment, Oliver knew—love was the greatest gift of all: a gift not just to feel, but to share, and one that would always be with him.

Printed in Great Britain
by Amazon

57323262R00057